OPERATION
CATFLAP

by
Peter Tye

Illustrations
Mike Cowdrey

FOR

Elias Cowdrey
who loves birds.
Or at least he did at the
age of two and three-quarters,
when this story was illustrated
by his grandfather.

WITH THANKS TO

Myfanwy Everett
Patient and diligent proof reader.

Marc Heraud
Press-ganged cover designer

Mike Cowdrey
Voluntary illustrator, who
went into deep shock on learning
how many pieces of artwork would
be required and the deadline.

TO THE MEMORY OF
Mandy
Mandy was a neighbour's fluffy &
chatty, brown hen. Often seen in deep
conversation with our shared robin.

Children's stories by Peter Tye

Operation Cat Flap
Splodge City
Badman: The Ghost of King John
Bee keeping for Cats
Crocodile Tours : Poking fun at a Pharaoh
Toliman the Barn Owl

Little Red Tractor
A White Christmas on Gosling Farm-
The Day of Molehills and Windmills
The Day Auntie Ellie went for a Swim
The Day Stan's World Turned Upside Down
The Day of the Big Surprise
The Ghost of Whistling Bridge
The Day Hetty went to Wrigglesworth
The Day Dudley was Late
The Day of the Shipwreck
The Day Puppy found his Name

The Prince with a Musical Bottom
(e-book only)

Abhilasha's Looking Glass
(Screen Play)

PROLOGUE

Camber House is a modest Georgian property. It was built for Doctor Cornelius Camber in 1798. Today it is owned by James Cornelius Camber, a retired engineer. James, who prefers to be called Jim, shares the house with his daughter Janet, who prefers to be called Jan. Her husband Michael, prefers to be called Mike and it was not long before their son, Leonard Cornelius, was called Leo. Leo calls his grandfather, 'Grandpa Jim' and as you are about to discover, so do most of the birds in the rambling garden.

CHAPTER ONE

A PRESENT WITH STRINGS

In the early hours of a winter morning, a bedroom door in Camber House, creaked open and a dark shape crept stealthily into the room

Green eyes danced in the soft glow of a night- light as Monty, the family cat, checked on the boy. He was fast asleep.

Monty followed a well-worn path around the bottom of the bed to a chair by the window. Using the chair as a step, he eased himself up onto the window ledge and disappeared behind the curtains.

A few minutes earlier, Monty had been curled up in his bed by the Aga. It was always warm. A marvellous invention!

He pretended to be asleep as Grandpa Jim crept through the kitchen, lighting his way with a small, but powerful torch, strapped around his woolly hat. Through half- closed eyes, Monty watched him take his coat off a hook on the back of the door, shrug into it, unlock the door and step out into the garden. A blast of ice-cold air swept into the kitchen, telling Monty all he wanted to know. He would not follow the old man. He would satisfy his curiosity by spying on him from the warmth of Leo's bedroom.

Monty peered out through the bedroom window. Lights were on in the workshop and the door was open. Grandpa Jim was busy carrying out the wooden frames he had been working on and stacking them against the outside wall. The rest of the garden was in darkness, but of course, that made no difference to Monty. He watched as Grandpa Jim carefully selected one of the frames and set off with it across the lawn. Where was he taking it? Suddenly, as so often happened, Leo's spaceship blocked his view. The boy insisted on building it on the window ledge where it could point towards the stars and Monty could understand that, but it made it difficult for him to move from one end of the window ledge to the other. The only way was to pass on the outside, which called for fine judgment. He achieved this by carefully placing his paws in line along the outer edge and moving the tip of his tail from side to side to keep balance. He had done it countless times before, but on this occasion, probably because he was in a hurry, his tail moved a fraction too far to the right.

It curled around the top of of the space ship and sent it crashing to the floor.

Leo was awake in an instant and a couple of seconds later, his mother burst into the room. She switched on the main light and they both saw a guilty-looking cat, jump out from behind the curtains and bolt out through the door. Leo's mother pointed to the floor underneath the window.

"Monty's knocked your spaceship over. Didn't I say it would be safer on the table in the living room?"

Leo got out of bed and looked down at the bricks scattered across the floor. The astronaut had parted company from the space-ship and looked surprised to find itself sprawled on a carpet; not floating in outer space. "I can soon build it again, mum," he said, as he parted the curtains to look out. "What was Monty doing up here anyway?"

Leo's mother quickly crossed the room and closed the curtains.

"You're not to look, Leo. Grandpa is working on something very special. He'll tell you about it later, you won't want to spoil the surprise." She helped him on with his dressing gown. "It's warm and cosy in the kitchen, let's have a hot drink and cook some breakfast."

Leo followed his mother down the stairs, wondering what Grandpa Jim was up to. He had been preparing a base for a shed on the edge of the lawn, but that would hardly be a surprise.

Monty's first thought when he scampered down the stairs was to make for one of his hiding places, but curiosity led him out through his cat flap towards the workshop. He stopped and laid low to watch Grandpa Jim carry the frames over to a patch he had been digging on the edge of the lawn. As a cat he took a keen interest in the finely raked soil, but before he could make use of it, it was completely covered with something which looked like grass, but wasn't. It was too spiky!

He watched patiently as Grandpa Jim stood two of the sections up on the green spiky stuff and bolted them together.

Working quickly he added more frames to the structure and after bolting on the last one, walked back towards the workshop.

It was beginning to get light. Monty crouched as low as he could in his hiding place, but the old man laughed as he turned towards him.

"It's no good trying to hide, Monty. Your tail's a dead give-away."

Monty looked over his shoulder to check his tail.

"Waving around like a flag stick," chuckled Grandpa Jim.

Monty got up, walked over and rubbed against the old man's legs. Grandpa Jim put a hand down and stroked his head.

"Don't worry, Monty we love you the way you are. My birds can see you coming from a mile away."

Monty watched Grandpa Jim carry more pieces over to where he had been working and join them together. Eventually Grandpa Jim told him it was time for breakfast so he followed him through the back door into the kitchen. But, fearing he could still be in trouble for knocking over the spaceship, he sprinted upstairs to one of his hiding places

"So what is it you're making, grandpa? Mum said it's a secret."

Grandpa Jim's blue eyes twinkled under white shaggy eyebrows as he looked across the kitchen table at Leo. He finished a mouthful of porridge before replying.

"It's a secret we were going to keep until Christmas Day, but unfortunately there has to be a change of plan. After breakfast I'll need Mum's help, so if you come out with us, I can tell you all about it.

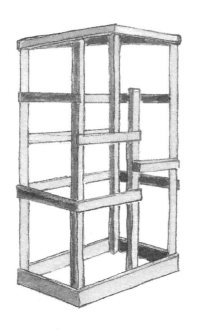

When Leo went into the garden, he could see that Grandpa Jim had been very busy. There was a structure where he said he was going to build a shed, but it did not look much like a shed. Then there was a post in the ground towards the shrubbery, where he fed his birds and it had an old bike wheel, without a tyre, on the top. That was very strange.

Grandpa Jim smiled at him. "What do you think it's going to be?"

Leo scratched his head. "I don't know Grandpa, but it doesn't look much like a shed."

Grandpa Jim laughed. "I should hope not. Let's go to my workshop, there are a few more bits to fit on. See if you can guess what it is as we go along."

Leo watched as his mother and grandpa carried a wooden frame across the lawn and propped it up against the structure. As Grandpa Jim used his electric screwdriver to secure it in place, Leo yelled with delight.

"Got it! It's a climbing frame!"

"Spot on," beamed Grandpa Jim, before adding, "well, that's what it's supposed to be. It was to be a surprise for Christmas. Your dad was going to help me put it up on Christmas Eve, but as you know, his work means he can't be here.

I've put it up today because my sister, that's your Great Aunt Libby, is having an operation and I'm leaving tomorrow to look after her."

"You mean, you won't be here for Christmas either?" asked a shocked Leo.

"Not sure," said Grandpa Jim, patting him on the shoulder. "But there is another reason for putting it up early. I want you to do something very important for me."

They were back in the workshop standing by a strange looking contraption on the workbench. It had a roof and suspended under the roof, another bike wheel, with the tyre removed.

"We shall have to be careful with this one, Janet."

Wow! thought Leo, this must be something special. Grandpa Jim only called his mum, Janet, if it was something serious. He looped what look like black rope over his shoulder and on his instruction, they both lifted the contraption and carried it carefully out through the door. It fitted on the climbing frame to make a sort of tower and after making some adjustments, Grandpa Jim looped the black rope, which turned out to be a rubber chain, around the bike wheel. Then he climbed a ladder propped up against the post and looped it around the other bike wheel. He grinned at Leo.

"Now, all will be revealed," he said mysteriously.

Grandpa Jim led Leo to where his bird feeders were hanging from branches in the shrubbery.

"All the birds rely on me for food during the winter and this December is forecast to be one of the coldest on record. Your mum is going to be very busy in the run-up to Christmas, so I'm relying on you to feed the birds for me. But there is a problem. Can you see what it is?"

He reached up to unhook a bird feeder from a branch and nodded to Leo to do the same. Leo stood on tip toes and stretched a hand up towards another bird feeder. "I can't reach, Grandpa."

"Of course you can't," he said kindly. "You're a big boy, but you are only seven years old."

"Seven and a quarter," said Leo.

"I stand corrected," said Grandpa Jim, "but I've thought of a way to make it easy for a boy who is seven and a quarter to reach the bird feeders Let's see if my plan works."

On the way back to the climbing frame, Grandpa Jim hooked the bird feeder he had taken down onto the rubber chain.

"Now Leo. I want you to climb the frame, stand under the wheel and turn that handle."

"The thing in the middle of the wheel?"

"That's it. I took it off the old bike, it's one of the peddles. Turn it anti-clockwise."

Leo slowly turned the handle.

"Great!" Shouted Grandpa Jim. "It's working. You can turn it faster if you like."

As Leo turned the wheel, the rubber chain brought the bird feeder towards him.

"Stop!" shouted Grandpa Jim. "Can you reach it now?"

"Easy." said Leo, who found the bottom of the feeder level with his chest.

"Can you unhook it?"

Using both hands, Leo unhooked the feeder and turned towards Grandpa Jim with a triumphant grin.

"Jolly good," said Grandpa Jim. "Now, put it on the floor and see if you can open the top and pour some of this in." He handed Leo a bag of bird seed. Leo did as instructed and without any prompting, hooked the feeder back on.

Grandpa Jim and Leo's mother cheered and clapped their hands. "Well done!" said Grandpa Jim. "The feeder should be able to go around the wheel without getting snagged, so turn the handle the same way and see what happens. Stop turning when the feeder is about halfway back towards the

pole, then wait until mum and I get back."

When Leo had the feeder in the right position he turned his attention to the workshop.

Sophie and Cressida, his mother's

large brown hens, were peering in through the door.

The hens flapped their wings and squawked as Grandpa Jim came out backwards, holding one end of something which was bright-red and shiny. His mother emerged holding the other end and as they turned to walk it sideways across the lawn,

Leo could see that it was a slide.

Feeding the birds was going to be fun!

Sophie and Cressida clucked their approval as Grandpa Jim bolted the top end of the slide to the climbing frame.

Then, Leo used it to join his mother, Grandpa Jim and the hens to admire his early Christmas present.

"So, do you think you'll be able to feed the birds while grandpa's away?"

"Sure thing, Mum. It's going to be great fun."

"Nothing wrong with it being fun," said Grandpa Jim. "But remember, we're in for some very cold weather and the birds will be relying on you."

"I won't let you down, grandpa."

"It's not me you would be letting

down," said Grandpa Jim, "it would be the birds." He pointed at the feeder. "Look! There's your first customer."

It's the robin," whispered Leo.

"Rob's always first," chuckled Grandpa Jim. "Here, Rob!" He put his hand in a pocket and pulled out a dried meal worm.

The robin flew over, took the worm from his hand and flew up to watch them from the roof of the climbing frame.

"Is his name really Rob?" asked Leo.

"Must be," said Grandpa Jim with a grin, "he always comes when I call. You try." He pulled another meal worm from his pocket and gave it to Leo, who stretched his hand out towards the robin.

"Here, Rob." The robin looked down at him.

"Here Rob." The robin tilted its head suspiciously to one side.

"Don't worry," said Grandpa Jim, "keep it in your pocket and try later. You'll have to be patient and earn his trust. In the meantime, let's get some more feeders."

Leo went with Grandpa Jim, while his mother went to the kitchen for more bird food.

When there were five feeders hanging in a neat row between the climbing frame and the post, Grandpa Jim patted Leo on the shoulder. "Well done, now all we have to do is think of something to call it? It's a bit more than a climbing frame, don't you think?"

"More like a bird station," said Leo, as more birds found the feeders.

"That's very good," said mum. "How about calling it Leonard's Bird Station?"

Grandpa Jim smiled. "I think Leo's Bird Station would be better,"he chuckled, "that should attract birds from miles around."

CHAPTER TWO

SECOND THOUGHTS

News travels fast amongst birds and within minutes all of those in easy flying distance of Camber House, knew Grandpa Jim was going away.

Coming on top of a weather warning given to Mr Crow, by a passing seagull, they were all very worried. Arctic conditions from the North Pole were spreading across the country. It would be icy-cold for weeks, perhaps even months. Grandpa Jim was their lifeline, without his help, many of the birds would not survive.

After investigating the new position of their feeders, the birds assembled on wires and in shrubs and trees to watch glumly as Grandpa Jim put Leo through his paces.

He found an old rucksack to make it easier for Leo to carry the different packs of birdseed from the kitchen, across the lawn, up the ladder and onto what the birds heard Grandpa Jim refer to as, Leo's Bird Station. As the training progressed, the birds began to feel happier and when Leo brought out food for the bigger birds and spread it out on the table under the canopy, blackbirds, thrushes, jackdaws, starlings and a pair of turtle doves, nodded to each other in relief. But a pessimistic pigeon pointed out that Leo was treating it like a game.

"What about when he comes home tired after a day at school?" he moaned. "It won't be a game then, it'll be a chore and children don't like chores."

The following morning, the birds found that more food had been put out after they went to roost. The pessimistic pigeon, who the other birds called, 'Pessie' said it must have been put out by Grandpa Jim. A light frost crisped the longer tufts of grass on the lawn, but that was nothing compared to what they could expect when the Arctic weather arrived. What if Pessie was right? They all stopped feeding to watch Grandpa Jim put a suitcase in the boot of his car and listened to the final instructions he gave to his grandson.

"Good work, Leo. I went to put more food out yesterday evening after the birds went to roost, but found you had beaten me to it! Well done, it really is very important. The birds will be up long before you and when it's been freezing all night, they need to start eating as soon as possible."

"I won't forget Grandpa. I'll look after the bird-bath too. I broke the ice with the hammer you gave me this morning."

"Good boy." Grandpa Jim gave Leo a hug. "If I can't get back in time, have a good Christmas and don't forget to keep an eye open for Santa Claus."

Leo laughed. "Really grandpa, you know I'm too old for that sort of thing."

Grandpa Jim shrugged. "You're never too old," He reached into his jacket pocket and produced an old, well-thumbed, exercise book. "You may find this useful. It's a record of all the birds I saw in this garden when I was a boy. It was during a cold winter like this threatens to be." He reached into another pocket and produced a new note book. "Write down the names of the birds that visit your bird station in here. Drawings of them would be nice. We can go through them together when I get back."

As Grandpa Jim shut the boot of his car the boy's mother came out from the house to say goodbye. The birds knew her as Janet and Mr Crow claimed to have watched her play in the garden as a young girl. She was a kind person who looked after her hens very well, but left the wild birds to grandpa Jim. Perhaps Janet would step in and help Leo take care of them?

Grandpa Jim waved and shouted as he drove away "DON'T FORGET. FEED THOSE BIRDS!"

Leo kept waving until Grandpa Jim's car disappeared from sight. As he reluctantly followed his mother into the house to get ready for school, the birds began to assemble in the beech tree to hold a 'Cold Weather Survival Meeting'.

As a bird who had survived more severe winters than any of the others, Mr Crow came down to to join them and a handsome song thrush chaired the meeting. He held up a wing for silence and looked hard at the blue tits and sparrows until they stopped twittering.

"Welcome to the meeting, we all know why it has been called, so there's no need for an agenda. But, before we begin,

I'm sure you will all want to join me in wishing Leo's Great Aunt Libby a speedy recovery from her operation."

A lady blackbird aggressively pushed her way to the front. "We couldn't care less about Great Aunt Libby! It's Grandpa Jim going away that's bothering us."

The song thrush looked at her nervously. "Yes, Beryl, I was only trying to say..."

"Well, don't bother!" snapped the lady blackbird. "We don't have time for all that nonsense. An Arctic winter is on its way. Temperatures are about to plummet. Our main source of food has just scarpered and you want us to wish Great Aunt Libby a speedy recovery?"

Mr Crow hopped down a branch to intervene.

"Steady on Beryl. I'm sure Rupert meant that the sooner Great Aunt Libby recovers, the quicker we will see Grandpa Jim, or Grandpa Camber, as I prefer to call him, back in our midst." Beryl ruffled her feathers and turned for support from her mate, but Basil was no where to be seen.

A male blackbird was following Leo as he walked up the lane to catch the school bus.

It hid in the hedge by the bus stop and listened as Leo excitedly told a friend about his grandpa going away, his early Christmas present and how it would help him look after the birds in the garden. As he followed Emma, his friend, onto the school bus, the blackbird heard him invite her to help feed the birds when they came home from school.

Basil flew swiftly across the garden as the bus drove off. He wanted to give the good news to the other birds, but as he approached the beech tree he was met by an angry Beryl

"Where were you when I needed you, Basil? We're in danger of starving and you go gallivanting off to heaven knows where." She looked at him suspiciously. "You haven't got a secret stash of food?"

"Of course not, my dear, you know I share everything with you."

"Not worms you don't!"

"Only because it's too difficult, my sweet. Worms are slippery customers and have to be gobbled-up as quickly as possible, but I always direct you to where you might find one."

"Yes. Yes. Alright." said Beryl irritably. "So where have you been?"

"I followed Leo and overheard him talking to his friend, Emma. I have some very good news for the meeting."

When he told Beryl what he had seen and heard, she set off and beat him to the beech tree. When he squeezed in amongst the other birds, she had already relayed the news to the meeting.

"Well that's jolly good news," said Rupert. "I think we can all relax in the knowledge that Leo is enthusiastic about the task in hand."

"It's a long time to Christmas," said Pessie.

"Mark my words, he'll get bored and let us down."

"Give over, Pessie! We're on a winner!" shouted a sparrow. "If he brings a friend along, they'll treat it like playtime."

"Binkie's right," chorused a pair of long- tailed tits. "They'll throw seed around as if there's no tomorrow."

"But there is a tomorrow," moaned Pessie. "In fact, there could be over a month of tomorrows until Grandpa Jim comes back. Mark my words, Leo will get bored and forget us."

"Not if Rob has anything to do with it."

All eyes and beaks turned to Mr Crow.

"I mean it," he said. "Rob may not be top of the popularity stakes amongst birds, but as far as humans are concerned he's colourful and loveable."

"Hardly more colourful than me," protested a Goldfinch "and as  for being loveable, you're not talking about the same robin who wants all the food to himself are you, Mr Crow?"

 "I would consider myself at least equal in the plumage stakes and my bird-table manners are certainly a lot better than Rob's," said a bullfinch.

Mr Crow spread his wings in an all encompassing gesture. "I agree with you Bertie. I agree with you Goldie, but would you be bold enough to take food from a human's hand? I suggest not, but Rob will."

"Oi! This is me they're talking about!" A robin flew up onto the branch next to Rupert the song thrush. "Come on Roop, you're supposed to be in charge, call the meeting to order!"

"Or you'll do what? Peck his blinking eyes out!"

Connie the coal tit's wicked impression of Rob had all the birds twittering with laughter. Rupert did his best not to twitter along with them and called the meeting to order. "Now then! Order! Come on folks, this is a serious matter."

"You bet it's a serious matter," scowled Rob. "What's the silly old crow on about?"

Mr Crow shrugged. "I have to admit to being old, Rob. I've looked over the garden from the top of this Beech tree for close on thirty years, but I am definitely not silly, far from it. I have observed and know all bird traits and I can say, most definitely, that the Camber family have been delighted when they have had a robin in their garden bold enough to take food from a human hand." Mr Crow paused and looked at his audience. "Our current robin, as rough a diamond as you may think he is, delights Grandpa Camber, or Grandpa Jim, as you prefer to call him, every time he perches on his hand to take a meal worm or some other titbit. I firmly believe. No, I know, that the demonstration of trust by Rob and his kin, has cultivated a sense of duty in the Camber family when it comes to feeding all the birds."

"That's not trust. That's greed!" shouted a blue tit.

Rob turned on him.

"What d'you know about it, Charlie? Ya spend most of yer time upside down. Keep yer beak out!" He turned back to face Mr Crow. "So, if I reads what you're sayin', you want me to take food from the boy's hand? You expect me to trust a kid? Kids are unpredictable. I prefers to give 'em a wide berth."

"Don't we all, Rob," said a wren as she hopped onto a twig near the robin. "But if it helps all of us, it would be a nice thing to do. Something for us to tell your mate, in the spring; when she comes back into the garden."

Rob looked at her for a few seconds before replying. "Small and crafty, that's what you are, Gwen Wren. Okay, I'll do it. I'll take food from the boy's hand, but, if it don't work, you can all blame Mr Crow."

****

When Leo brought his friend Emma into the garden after school, they had great fun using the bird station to fill all the feeders. The robin was close by and Leo suddenly remembered the meal worm he had in his pocket. He showed it to Emma.

"The robin takes these from grandpa's hand. He told me it would take time but if I gain the robin's trust, Rob will take it from me." He held his hand out and called to the robin. "Here Rob, Grandpa Jim gave me this for you."

To Leo's amazement, the robin flew across, perched on his thumb and gently tugged out the meal worm.

"Wow!" murmured Leo.

"Fantastic!" whispered Emma. "Can I have a go."

"We'll have to get some meal worms," said Leo, "I know where grandpa keeps them, come on!"

Emma followed Leo down the slide and ran after him to the house, where an excited Leo told his mother what had happened. When they went back to the bird station, Emma tried to feed the robin, but without success.

After a few days, Emma had other things to do and could not help Leo feed the birds, but Leo did not mind. Every time he went out to his Bird Station, the robin would magically appear and perch on his hand to take a meal worm.

A week after Grandpa Jim left, the arctic weather arrived. Overnight the temperature dropped way below freezing and stayed that way. Leo found that the hammer would not break ice in the bird bath and his mother showed him how to thaw it with warm water.

The birds were struggling but took comfort in the knowledge that like Grandpa Jim, Leo would look after them. But, after a heavy fall of snow, the school bus could not get through and with the Christmas holiday break only a few days away, the decision was taken to close the school. The children were delighted, but it created a problem for Leo's mother who, having followed the family tradition, side-stepped by Grandpa Jim, had to juggle her part time hours as a doctor,

Emma's mother came to the rescue and Leo spent the day with them. The birds were seeing less of him and in a rush to get to Emma's, he was only partly filling the feeders. Then, one morning, after forgetting to put out food the previous evening, he only filled one.

The birds waited anxiously by Leo's Bird Station all day.

They desperately wanted some food before they went to roost, but when Leo came home, his mother had some news for him.

It was good news. Great Aunt Libby was recovering well and Grandpa Jim was hoping she would be fit enough to travel and join them for Christmas. Leo was so excited he forgot about the birds and settled down to watch 'Toy Story', which Grandpa Jim bought for his third Christmas. They often watched it together and Leo remembered all the bits that made Grandpa Jim chuckle and felt warm and happy.

When his mother came out from her study and found him asleep on the settee. She switched off the television and took him up to bed.

CHAPTER THREE

THE STRANGE VISITOR

Leo was dreaming and in his dream, he was one of the toys in the film. As he could not see himself, he did not know which toy, but he was following Woody, the toy cowboy, on an adventure. It was all very exciting and eventually, Woody led all the toys back through the window into the nursery. Then, the dream began to go wrong! Woody and all the toys were inside celebrating the success of their adventure but he was outside, on the window sill, looking in. It was very cold. He tapped on the window and shouted. "Let me in! Let me in!" It began to snow. He banged on the window and yelled at the top of his voice. "Let me in! Let me in! It's cold out here!"

Leo woke-up with a start! The duvet had slipped off the bed and he was cold. He switched on the bedside lamp and pulled the duvet back into position. "Phew! What a dream!" He snuggled down again and was reaching to switch off the light when he heard something tapping on the window. It tapped again, only this time much louder, more like a rap. Then a voice shouted.

"Let me in! It's cold out here!"

Leo sat up. He knew that voice? It was Woody the toy cowboy from the movie! He slipped out of bed, crept over to the window and carefully parted the curtains.

There was nothing there. "Must have been dreaming," he muttered to himself, as he turned to go back to bed. "Strange dream though." Then, he heard the voice again!

"Come on! Come on! Open up, it's cold out here!"

"Whose th- th- there?" asked Leo.

"Me," said the voice.

"Who's m-m-me?

"Santa Claus," said the voice.

Santa Claus?" queried Leo. "There's no such person as Santa Claus."

"Suit yourself," said the voice, "but let

me in, it's freezing out here!"

Leo looked through the curtains again, but all he could see was his own reflection in the window.

"Not up there, down here!"

Leo looked down. There was a strange bird, perched on the window sill, looking in at him!

"Come on dude," said the bird. "Open the

window and let me in, it's mighty cold out here."

"Are you Woody from Toy Story?" asked Leo.

"No, I told you, I'm Santa Claus," said the bird.

"You sound just like Woody," said Leo, cautiously opening the window.

The bird stepped through and struck a pose. "Ta - rah! Told you it was Santa Claus!"

As the bird moved into the light, its feathers shimmered, shone and projected colours around the room.

"You're not Santa Claus and you're definitely not Woody," said Leo "but wow! I've never seen a bird like you before."

"D'ya like it?" asked the bird, twirling around and slowly moving its wings up and down. "This is my winter outfit. I like to shine in the winter months, it cheers people up."

"Well, you really do shine. Those colours are dazzling. Who are you? What are you?"

The bird put in a couple of extra twirls and moved its wings, which flashed and twinkled. "When you said my colours were dazzling, you almost had it, Leo. I'm a Razzdazz Oriole, what else could I be?"

"I don't know," said a bemused Leo.

"You're incredible! You're fantastic, but where does a Razzdazz ..... what ever your name is, come from? I've never seen one in the garden."

The birds beak tweaked into a smile. "Razzdazz Oriole's a bit of a mouthful, you can call me Razz, most folks do. I'm from thee land of the midnight sun, but that's only in the summer. In the winter the sun hardly ever shines, that's when I trade in my yellow and black feathers for this reflective little number."

Leo reached out to touch a dazzling surface, which turned out to be one of many mirrors hinged together. The beak was bright orange, but it was difficult to see where it finished because the small mirrors on the bird's head reflected orange, almost up to the eyes, which were royal blue. The mirrors across the bird's belly and down the legs where they joined deep purple claws, were about the same size, but those running down the back to the tail and on the wings were much bigger.

"How do you manage to fly? asked Leo. "Those mirrors must be very heavy?"

"No, light as a feather," said the bird with a chuckle. "They're a perfect fit and they're snow-proof, water-proof, fire-proof and every other kind of proof you could care to mention. On top of that, they're so smooth I can slip though the air more quickly than I could with feathers. There is one problem though."

"And what's that?" asked Leo.

The bird tapped on the surface of a mirror, with its bright orange beak. "In a word, condensation. When I come into a warm room like this, the mirrors mist up. You haven't got a duster I could borrow have you Leo? A handkerchief will do, as long as you don't have a runny nose. Failing that, do you have a reasonably clean sock?"

Leo was more confused than ever. What was he doing talking to a bird with mirrors for feathers? A Razzdazz Oriole who

preferred to be called Razz, claimed to be Santa Claus and wanted to borrow a sock to wipe away some condensation? It just had to be another dream. But this one seemed so real? Cold air coming in through the open window made him shiver. He hugged his arms and felt goose bumps. He pinched himself and felt a sharp pain. The bird was watching him. "No, you're
not dreaming," it said. Then an unblinking eye fixed on Leo and try as he might, he could not look away.

The bird's eye seemed to be getting bigger.

Pictures appeared, welling up from the dark depths of the iris. There were scenes of cities, the countryside the sky and the sea. They overlapped creating confusion. They pulsated and glowed and started to spin. Leo found himself drawn towards the eye. His feet left the ground. He put his hands out to stop himself, but he was drawn into the whirling mass.

He felt giddy and called out, "Razz! Please help me Razz!" but the whirling only got quicker! Then he was tumbling and falling. Falling, into a black hole.

Leo closed his eyes as he hurtled head first, down into the darkness. Then, he heard Razz calling to him.

"Put your arms out Leo, quickly boy. Put them out. Now!"

Leo spread his arms and the downward rush was immediately turned into a forward motion and then upward. Up and up! It was like going up in a super-fast lift!

"Over here Leo. Point yourself over here."

Leo opened his eyes. It was very dark, but he thought he could make out a brick wall and it looked as if he was going to go slap bang into it! "Up a bit and over to your left," called Razz. Looking up, Leo saw Razz in the open window. He pointed himself in that direction, but he was too low and on a collision course with the window sill!

"Use your arms." instructed Razz, but with a crash only a split second away, Leo had no time to take any advice. He stuck his feet out to cushion the inevitable impact and seemed to hang in mid-air!

"Watch it or you'll stall!"

Leo's head was level with the sill; he put his arms out to grab hold of something, the curtains, the window frame, the sill, anything would do. But his hands would not work. They would not, they could not, grab hold of anything. His arms were sliding off the sill when the strange bird came to his rescue. With one purple foot hanging onto the window frame, it grabbed Leo with the claws of the other. With a mighty heave Razz pulled and Leo felt a sharp pain in his shoulder as he was bundled through the window.

Leo lay on his back on the window ledge. He was out of breath and out of danger, but feeling very strange. The Razzdazz Oriole was looking down at him, holding a brown feather in its beak.

"Sorry about that," it said, "but you will be able to fly perfectly well without it."

"What do you mean f-fly?" stuttered Leo. "I can't fly."

"Sure you can fly," said the bird. "What do you think you've been doing? Waving to the milkman? Mind you we are going to have to work on your technique. Your take-off needs to become second nature and your landings a matter of pin-point accuracy. Of course the fun starts when you progress to loops and barrel rolls. Yes, Leo, we're going to work on your flying because....."

"Just a minute, just a minute!" interrupted Leo, as he struggled to get to his feet. "What makes you think I want to learn to fly at all?"

The Razzdazz oriole opened its beak and dropped the brown feather.

It floated down and rested for a few seconds on the window ledge before the cold air from the open window wafted it into the room. The feather gently see-sawed its way to the floor, which seemed a long way down.

"Is that really my bedroom floor?" thought Leo. He looked across the room towards the bed. The room looked familiar, but enormous. When he turned to look through the window he was only just tall enough to peer over the window frame. He looked up at Razz, who was now at least three times taller than himself!

"Confusing, ain't it?" said Razz. "You see, what I am trying to say is that you're going to learn to fly, because you're built for it. Come on, hop over here and take a look at yourself."

Leo followed Razz along the window ledge until they drew level with the closed part of the window. Leo could see the brightly coloured bird reflected in the window, but as they moved further along there was something else. It was a smudge of red. Leo moved forward to take a closer look. Ah, now he could see it properly, it was another bird. It was a robin. A robin with ruffled feathers on its right shoulder.

"Ornithology," said Razz.

"Beg your pardon?" said Leo. "What's ornithology?"

"Ornithology is the scientific study of birds," replied Razz, "though just how a bird can scientifically study itself beats me."

"You mean I'm looking at myself?

"You sure are."

Leo moved forward and touched the window with his nose. At the same time, the robin moved forward and rested its beak against the window.

Leo tapped the window with his nose.

The robin tapped back with its beak.

Leo turned his head to one side.

The robin turned its head to one side.

Leo stood on one leg.

The robin stood on one leg.

Leo raised his arms.

The robin raised its wings.

Leo moved his arms up and down.

The robin moved its wings up and down.

Leo's feet lifted off the window ledge and at the same time, the robin started to fly up the window. The faster Leo moved his arms, the higher they both went.

Leo stopped moving his arms and put them down by his side and both he and the robin dropped into an undignified heap.

"Never do that!" shouted Razz. "Never, ever, fold your wings away until you've made a safe landing!"

"Gosh," said a dazed Leo as he scrambled to his feet. "It really is me. I really am a bird! I'm a robin!"

Leo held up one wing and then the other. Then he turned to look over his shoulder for a back view.

"Are you happy as a robin?" asked Razz. "I can turn you into any bird you wish. It does mean repeating all that through the eye stuff though."

"No, no, I'm quite happy to be a robin," said Leo quickly. "If I have to be a bird at all that is. Why have you turned me into a bird Razz?"

"Do it to a child every time I visit your quaint little old country," replied Razz. "Especially to children who have broken a promise to feed the birds."

"Crikey, the birds! I forgot to put anything out last night. I am sorry."

"So are the birds," said Razz. "They're starving."

"I'll put something out when I get up, I promise," said Leo.

"Unless you forget."

"I won't forget, I really do promise."

"Too late for more promises," said Razz. "I'm going to show you how much the birds in your garden rely on you for food. Especially in a cold winter like this."

"I would much rather you turned me back into a boy," said Leo.

"Don't worry," said Razz. "I'll turn you back, I always do."

"But what if you're out of practice,"

asked Leo. "When was the last time you turned someone into a bird?"

Razz thought hard for a few seconds. "Let me see now. Hmmm, yes. Last time I was here was 1964. Time before that it was '47. Hard winter for birds, '47. Then there was '34....or was it '35?"

"A-ha, now I know it!" interrupted Leo.

"Know what?"

"Know I'm dreaming," said Leo.

"And how do you work that out?" asked Razz.

"Because, you said you were here in 1934 or 1935 and everyone knows birds don't live that long," said Leo triumphantly.

"This bird does," said Razz quietly. "But I was getting mixed up. I was here in '35, but it was 1835 not 1935."

"Huh! said Leo. "I knew it, I am dreaming. I'll wake up in a minute. I'll be my old self again and you'll have gone."

The bird sighed. "You have a lot to do and a lot to learn before you get back to your old self, Leo. Don't you believe in magic, boy?"

"Not really," said Leo. "I mean, there's always a trick behind it isn't there? Like sawing a lady in half, or putting someone in a box and making them vanish. They're all tricks, they're not real magic."

"They're illusions," replied Razz.

"Tricks. Illusions. You can call them what you like. There's no such thing as real magic" said Leo, confident now that he really was dreaming.

"Is that right?" said Razz, looking down his beak at Leo. "And from what you said earlier, I gather you don't believe in Santa Claus either?"

"Of course not, that's kids' stuff!"

"And how old are you, kid?" asked

Razz.

"Seven and a quarter," replied Leo proudly.

"Seven and a quarter?" said Razz. "And you don't believe in magic, or in Santa Claus. Well, there's nothing else for it. Christmas is only a short time away and you've got a lot of believing to catch up on." Razz shuffled along the window ledge, nudging Leo towards the open window.

"After you, little robin," he said, as he gave Leo a push. This time, Leo instinctively spread his wings and flew in a series of uncertain swoops, down to his bird station.

CHAPTER FOUR

THE COLD GARDEN

Leo landed half way up the sloping roof of his bird station, which was covered with frost. Razz flew in expertly and nudged him up the slippery slope so that he could get a firm footing on the ridge. He could just make out the dark shape of the Camber House roof as Razz fluttered up to join him.

"Well done," he said, "how are you feeling?"

"Very strange," answered Leo. "In fact, to be honest, I feel a bit scared."

"That's understandable," said Razz. "But, not wishing to be unkind, you have brought this on yourself."

"I think I've learnt my lesson, Razz. If you take me back to my room and turn me back into a boy, I'll bring food out for the birds. I promise."

"Sorry, Leo, but the only way to truly learn your lesson is to experience how hungry the birds really are. Now, first things first. You managed to glide down here, but you need some flying lessons"

"Couldn't I have something to eat? I'm starving!"

"Aren't we all," said Razz, "but work first. If you can fly properly, you'll find it easier to feed yourself......and get out of trouble!"

"But I'm cold," whined Leo.

"Puff your feathers out, that'll help" said Razz. "Ah, here comes your flying instructor, Bertie Bullfinch."

A splendid bullfinch flew down and landed near them.

"Morning Bertie," said Razz, "how are you today?"

"Wing's a bit painful, Razz," replied the bullfinch. "Always the same when it's very cold."

"Sorry to hear it." Razz explained to Leo that Bertie was caught mid-flight by a sparrow hawk and was lucky to get away with his life."

"Took on more than he bargained for," said Bertie fiercely, but added, wistfully, "makes long distance flying a bit difficult though."

"Ah, but you're still one of the best instructors," said Razz. "I've got a new pupil for you. This is Leo, the boy from the house. I've put him on a bird familiarisation course. As you will know, Leo promised Grandpa

Jim he would put food out for the birds in the garden, but, at a time when you need it most, he has forgotten."

"Humph!"snorted Bertie. "Jolly bad show that, Leo."

"Bad show? Bad show? Disgusting more like! Absolutely disgusting!" Leo turned to see a plump lady blackbird perched on a branch in the apple tree. A slender male blackbird was next to her.

"Oh, I don't know Beryl my love," said

the male blackbird. "We had food yesterday."

The female blackbird, who was looking angrily at Leo, turned on her partner.

"Yesterday? Yesterday? It dropped to minus ten last night, Basil, and you talk about yesterday! What we had yesterday won't keep us going for another hour!"

"Well, perhaps we should go back to roost and conserve our energy," suggested Basil, rather nervously.

Beryl pushed her beak dangerously close to Basil's eye. "And what happens then, bird brain?"

Basil hopped sideways along the branch, but Beryl followed. "I'll tell you what happens," she said, before he had a chance to answer. "I'll tell you what happens. You get weak from lack of food; fall off your perch and it's bye, bye, Basil!"

A robin flew down to land expertly on the garden fork.

"It wouldn't be soon enough for me," he said. "Your darlin' Basil nicked one of my worms last week!" The lady blackbird turned her attention towards the robin.

"And just what makes you think all the worms in the garden belong to you Rob?"

"If they're in my territory, they're mine!" declared the robin. "Crumbs off the bird-table is one thing, worms and insects are another. You know the score you interfering old busybody, so just keep your beak out!"

"How dare you? How dare you?" hissed Beryl, her feathers ruffling with indignation. "Did you hear that Basil? Are you going to let him talk to me like that?"

Basil moved uneasily on the branch. "Now look here, Rob," he wheedled, "we're all in this together, you really should....."

"Should what?" interrupted Rob, leaning forward aggressively on the fork handle. "Should what? Come on, spit it out you silly old....." Rob stopped mid sentence and stared at Leo who tried to hide behind Razz.

"What? Who's this then? Another robin on my patch? I don't believe it. There he is, bold as brass, without so much as a by your leave, or sorry, but I lost my way." Rob pointed across the garden with a wing.

"On yer way sunshine! Go on, make it sharp, before I has your eyes for breakfast!"

Leo was so shaken by this onslaught that he prepared to fly off, but Razz put out a restraining wing. "Steady on, Rob," he said soothingly. "This is not a real robin, this is Leo, the boy from the house." Rob immediately changed his aggressive stance.

"Beggin' yer pardon Razz," he said. "But he does look like the real thing."

"Well, I can assure you he's not," said Razz. "I've turned Leo into a robin to teach him a lesson. He promised Grandpa Jim he would put food out for the birds until he returned, but then, he was distracted and forgot."

"In that case, he does deserve to have his eyes pecked out!" muttered Rob gruffly.

"I really don't think that would solve anything Rob," said Bertie.

"No, I think it would be going much too far," said Basil.

"Trust Rob to suggest something like that," added Beryl, sweetly.

"Of course it demonstrates a complete lack of breeding. What I say is; we should pull all his feathers out, break his wings, then peck his eyes out!

"That's a much better idea," said Basil. "Oh, how clever you are, Beryl my dear."

These comments were greeted by a chorus of whistles, squeaks and squawks together with aggressive flapping.

Leo was surrounded by hostile birds. Razz flew in amongst them to calm things down. "Cool it folks! This is getting you nowhere fast. You have a serious food shortage on your wings. Let me spell it out to you. Read my beak! There - are - no - berries - left! The - ground - is - frozen - solid! The - bird feeders - are - empty and - there's nothing - on the - bird-table.

Taking it out on Leo won't solve anything. In the long run, he's going to be as good a friend to you as Grandpa Jim, you can take my word for it."

"Well of course, if you say so Razz, then we all believe you," said Rupert, the song thrush, squeezing in front of Beryl, anxious to establish his position as spokes-bird for the garden. "Isn't that right everyone?"

All the birds in the apple tree chorused their approval, but Rob still wasn't happy.

"That's all very well," he said, "but it don't change the fact that we're all hungry. Can't you use some of yer magic powers to conjure up some grub, Razz?"

"No, that would be abusing them," replied Razz. "Anyway, you ought to be checking other possibilities."

"Like what?" asked Rob.

"Like all the other gardens in the neighbourhood," said Razz. "What do you think Rupert?"

"Seems good to me, Razz." said Rupert. "We can fly off in groups to search in different directions. Beryl, if you and Basil could lead a group to the north. I'll lead to the south and Charlie, where's Charlie?"

Leo looked around to see who Charlie might be.

"Here!" said a voice from a high branch in a cherry tree.

In the dim light, Leo could just make out that the speaker was a chaffinch. On the same branch there were three great tits, a long row of blue tits, four long-tailed tits, two wagtails and a cluster of sparrows.

"If you could lead the small birds to the east please, Charlie," instructed Rupert. "Less flying time in that direction. Take the dunnocks with you, but keep an eye on them, you know what they're like for disappearing under shrubs and bushes, especially Danny."

Leo looked at the bottom of the shrub where Grandpa Jim said a dunnock would most likely be found, searching for insects. There was one there, busily scratching at the frozen soil. Was that Danny Dunnock? When the bird flew up to join the sparrows, he could see that some of them were indeed dunnocks. As he started to count them, his attention was caught by movement in a pear tree.

A large bird was shuffling along a bough, pushing four starlings and two collared doves along, squeezing a pigeon against the trunk.   "Help! I can't breath. I'm going to die! We're all going to die" gasped the pigeon.

"Hurry up and get on with it then, Pessie!" shouted Rob, "but we ain't gonna join ya! Keep pecking at Jack's toes, Connie! We'll be well rid of our Jonah."

A chorus of chirps and twitters from the cherry tree greeted Rob's remark, but Rupert was not amused.

"Who's Connie?" whispered Leo, as the song thrush told the robin not to be so rude.

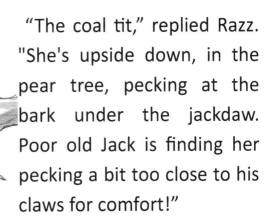

"The coal tit," replied Razz. "She's upside down, in the pear tree, pecking at the bark under the jackdaw. Poor old Jack is finding her pecking a bit too close to his claws for comfort!"

"Connie!" ordered Rupert. "There's nothing there for you, please join Charlie and the other small birds. We're going to search neighbouring gardens as Razz suggested. Could you lead the other birds to the west please Razz?"

"I don't see why not," said Razz, "but who's going to relay the news, if and when food is found?"

"Pessie will be best for that!" called Mr Crow. "I can watch everything from the top of my tree. When I see that food has been found, I will send him off in the appropriate direction. There's nothing faster than a pigeon for delivering news."

"Only when there's news to deliver," moaned Pessie. "They won't find any food. No chance."

"We have to live in hope," said Rupert. "If food is found, I can't think of any bird who could spread the good news quicker than you, Pessie."

"But not with a smile," chirped a sparrow.

All the small birds twittered. Rupert tilted his head to hide a grin and held up a wing.

"Thank you, Binkie. Now all form up behind your leaders and wait for Bertie's signal. We don't want everyone airborne at once, let's have an orderly departure with no collisions."

Leo saw flashes of colour as pairs of goldfinches, yellow hammers, goldcrests and greenfinches flew up to the bird station to perch behind Razz.

Razz turned to Leo. "Stay here while Bertie gets everyone started. He'll be back to give you some flying lessons. For your own safety, obey him at all times. If food is found he will lead you to it."

Leo nodded his understanding. He would do anything if it meant eating as soon as possible. He was starving!

CHAPTER FIVE

A ROBIN IN DANGER

Monty was missing Grandpa Jim. He was always up and about early. What with that and all the cold white stuff outside, Monty was feeling miserable. Nothing for it, to cheer himself up, he would go to Leo's room and snuggle up on his bed. He crept up the stairs, gave Janet's bedroom door a wide berth and moved silently along the landing to Leo's room. He pushed the door open and sauntered in.

What a shock!

It was freezing cold!

He was about to high-tail it back to the warmth of the kitchen, when he noticed Leo's duvet on the floor. Leo was not in his bed and cold air was blasting in through the window. He followed his usual path onto the window ledge to investigate. One side of the window was wide open and even before he peered out he could hear an unusual amount of bird activity in the garden.

Monty understood what humans were saying to him and to each other, but when it came to birds, he did not have a clue. All he heard were tweets and twitters, so he did not know that a bullfinch was saying "Ready for take-off," as it raised a wing, or that the reply from a lady blackbird was "ready" and the bullfinch shouted "FLY!" as it smartly dropped a raised wing

A group of birds took off in a flurry of beating wings and it was soon evident to Monty that they were heading in his direction. Not only that, they were led by the lady blackbird who made a habit of attacking him at every opportunity. Monty cowered away from the open window, but the birds soared upwards and northwards. When he looked out through the window again, the bullfinch was repeating the same procedure in front of different groups of birds and the sky was soon full of birds, flying off in all directions. When the action was over, there was only the bullfinch and one solitary robin in the garden. Time for him to go out and investigate.

Bertie the bullfinch stayed close to Leo as he flew in slow circles around the garden. He took him through the basics, before teaching him to quickly change direction, use his wings as air brakes and how to rotate them to hover. When Bertie's damaged wing caused him discomfort, he told Leo to fly as high as he could, then swoop down and land on the garden fork handle. He would be watching from the roof of the bird station. Full of confidence, Leo banked sharply away and flew higher. It was getting lighter and he could see the shape of the garden spread out below. He had a line on the garden fork and made a long fast dive towards it, swooping over the bird station, using his wings as air brakes and making what he considered to be a perfect landing on the fork handle.

The bullfinch watched Leo land. "Not bad for a beginner," he muttered, "but mustn't let the youngster get too full of himself."

So he bellowed. "Go round again. Approach too high and you rocked to maintain balance on landing."

"Seemed pretty good to me," said Leo cheekily.

"Don't argue with your instructor," snapped Bertie. "It was not good enough for me and that's what matters. Now, do another circuit. Jump to it!"

Leo flew round again........and again.....and again, with Bertie bullfinch shouting a torrent of instructions.

"Lift those wings up!"

"Fan that tail out!"

"Round again!"

"You're too high. Much too high!"

"Level out. Level out!"

"Hold those legs at an angle of 25 degrees."

"Make your approach from below the fork handle."

"I've seen better robins on a Christmas cake!"

It was mention of a Christmas cake which reminded Leo that he was starving.

"I wish they would hurry up and find some food," he moaned. "You don't think they've found some and kept it to themselves, do you?"

"Not a chance!" snorted the bullfinch. "Damnable impertinence! There is such a thing as honour amongst birds you know? If there's anything to be found, one of our birds will find it. When they do, we'll get the call. If you can't think of anything sensible to say, keep your beak shut."

Bertie was clearly very angry and Leo felt ashamed for having made such a suggestion. He looked down to avoid the cold gaze of the bullfinch and something on the ground caught his eye. He blinked. There was something. He flew down to check.

"Back on the fork that bird," ordered Bertie. But Leo was too engrossed to take any notice. He was investigating a crust of bread which had been trampled into the soil when it was wet. Now it was frozen solid. Could he get at it by pecking around the edges?

Bertie called out. "Leo, you're in danger down there. Fly back to the fork handle at once."

But Leo carried on pecking. "He's only upset because I saw it first," he told himself.

Bertie called out again. "There's a cat coming. Get off the ground quick. Fly boy! Fly!"

The urgent note in the bullfinch's
voice was enough to make Leo stop pecking

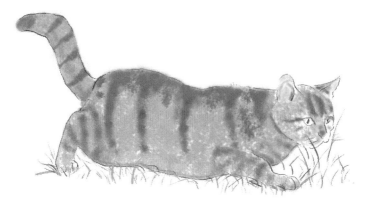

and look up. It was true, there was a cat
coming, a cat which was trying to keep low
to the ground, but it was not a hunter. It
was, Monty, his own cat. Monty never
caught birds, that was why Grandpa Jim
liked him so much.

He turned to carry on pecking at the
frozen crust of bread.

Monty stopped, and watched. That
interfering bullfinch had given him away.
The robin had seen him and yet? It was still

busily pecking at something by the garden fork.

In the four years of his life, Monty had never managed to catch a bird. He was laughed at by all the other cats in the neighbourhood. Was this his big chance? An instinct Monty never knew he had was taking over. The nervous excitement he normally felt at times like this had been replaced by a steely determination. He carefully gauged the distance to his intended victim and without even thinking about it, lowered his haunches and tail to the ground. Powerful muscles were readied for an explosive leap. Claws flicked out from their sheaths.

Prepared and deadly. Monty the pussy cat had turned into a killing machine!

Leo had almost freed one edge of the crust. Crumbs, but it was hard work being a bird. "Crumbs?" He giggled to himself, there was a joke there somewhere. He paused and glanced over towards Monty. His daft cat wanted to play.

"Hi Monty, it's me, Leo. I'm busy so go away, there's a good puss. Off you go, shooo!"

That was what Leo said, but what Monty heard was, "Tic tic, twitter twitter, tsit tsit, twitter twitter, tic tweet twitter, tswee."

Monty pounced!

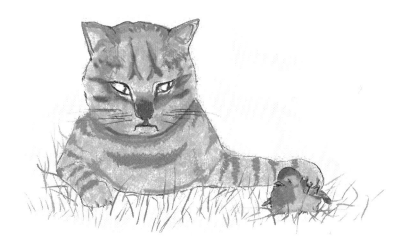

As his cat's outstretched paws pinned

him to the ground, Leo realised that Monty had not understood a word!

Leo shouted slowly and deliberately. "Let go, Monty! Let go! It's me, Leo! I've been turned into a robin, let me go!"

But, Monty enjoyed the robin's cries of distress. This was his big moment and he wanted to savour it. He would not kill the robin, not yet. He wanted to toy with it. He wanted to see the fear in its eyes. He wanted to do what he had seen other cats do, but most of all, he wanted another cat to come along and witness his great triumph.

Bertie overcame his initial shock and went into action. He flew straight at the cat, only pulling up to whistle between its ears at the very last moment. Monty ducked, but kept a firm hold on the robin. There was no way a demented old bullfinch was going to deprive him of his prize.

After several attacks, Bertie realised he was wasting time. The cat had Leo pinned firmly to the ground, but as far as he could see, there was no damage had been done. There was still hope, so forgetting his damaged wing; he flew swiftly to a great oak in a neighbouring garden and hovered near a hole, about half way up the trunk.

He was in dangerous territory so he shouted at the top of his voice. "Tanya! Tanya! We need your help! Tanya, please wake up! Tanya!"

"Are you looking for me?" said a

round, smooth, soothing voice.

Bertie looked up to see, Tanya, the tawny owl, perched on a bough about eight feet above the hole that was her home.

Keeping a respectful distance, Bertie flew to a nearby branch.

Tanya had her eyes closed. "How can I help yu-ooo?" she crooned.

"Something terrible has happened," replied Bertie

"I kno-ooow," said Tanya.

"A cat has caught a robin down by the bird-table."

"I kno-ooow."

"The robin's still alive."

"I kno-ooow"

"You are the only bird strong enough to rescue him."

"I kno-ooow," said Tanya. "I kno-ooow everything."

"Did you know that the robin is really

the boy Leo from the house?" asked Bertie.

Tanya opened one eye. "I think you are telling lies," she said, "but I don't give a hoot, I'll help you anyway."

The tawny owl opened her other eye, spread her huge wings and flew lazily across the garden. She hovered over Monty who looked up to see an owl dropping like a stone towards him. He let go of Leo to defend himself, but Tanya cleverly altered her angle of descent, brushed past his whiskers, scooped up Leo in her strong talons and with enormously powerful wings beating the air, lifted him swiftly out of Monty's reach.

Monty watched in disbelief as the owl flew back to the oak tree with his robin. Gone was the new found killer instinct, his shoulders drooped and he turned to slink away to the sanctuary of his cat flap.

The bullfinch was waiting in the oak tree when the owl returned.

"Jolly good show, Tanya. That was excellent, beautifully executed. Well done."

"I kno-ooow," said Tanya, landing

expertly on one leg, whilst clutching Leo firmly but safely in the talons of the other.

"Jolly good," repeated Bertie. "Jolly good, thank you very much. Thank you very much indeed."

The owl closed her eyes.

The bullfinch gave a nervous cough. "A hem. So, er, if you would just let Leo go, Tanya. I'm, er, sure he would like to thank you properly, um, then we shall be off and leave you in peace."

"I don't think so," crooned Tanya.

"You don't think so?" spluttered Bertie, "but why the devil not?"

"Because he's too young and inexperienced to be left with you," said Tanya silkily. "It will be much better if I take care of him."

"Hummph! I should never have trusted you!" snorted Bertie. "We all know how you take care of small birds."

"Oooooo-ooo, but I will," drooled Tanya. "Now go away while I have a little doze; before breakfast."

Leo heard everything and it didn't take him long to work out who was on the breakfast menu. Talk about out of the frying pan into the fire. Or in this case, out of the cat and into the owl!

He struggled to break free, but it was no use. Tanya looked down and blinked an eye, as if winking at him.

"No-ooow, why don't you have a little nap to-oooo," she said softly. "I won't let you fall, I promise. I'll take good care of you - such good care of yu-oooo."

Tanya closed her eyes, but Leo was too scared to even think about sleep. If only he had obeyed the bullfinch. But, where was the bullfinch? "Bertie! Bertie! Are you there Bertie?"

There was no reply. The bullfinch had deserted him!

CHAPTER SIX

THE MOBBING

Despite the pain in his damaged wing, Bertie was flying at full speed to give the alarm, but Mr Crow was already on the case. He had seen everything from the top of his beech tree and knew there was only one way to save Leo.

He sent Pessie to tell the others and set off to tell Rupert himself.

The song thrush was about half a mile south of Camber House when he saw Mr Crow diving swiftly towards him. He circled to shout the bad news.

"Tanya is holding Leo captive in her oak tree! She's having a nap, but could wake up at anytime. You'll have to organise a mobbing. Pessie is rounding up the others. Suggest you wait until everyone is in position before you start. If Tanya has time to get to her nest with Leo, all will be lost!"

Bertie was heading south to find Razz when he glimpsed a black shape diving towards him he was about to take cover in a hedge when Mr Crow called out. "Sorry to startle you, Bertie. Saw what happened to Leo. Have alerted Rupert who's on his way back to organise a mobbing. He'll need your help. Pessie is rounding up the others."

A relieved bullfinch headed for home and within a few minutes, Titch the goldcrest, Gene the greenfinch and Goldie the goldfinch caught up with him.

"Are we going to start the mobbing?" asked Goldie.

"No, we need a full turn out for that," said Bertie. "We'll watch Tanya and if she does wake up, we'll try to keep her talking."

Following Bertie's lead they landed carefully on an outer branch of the oak tree where they had a good view and, should it prove necessary, a clear flight path to her nest.

Tanya seemed to be in a deep sleep, but as Titch pointed out, the trouble with an owl is you never really know.

Connie the coal tit arrived and agitated for an immediate attack, but Bertie insisted they wait until all the birds arrived.

"There's safety in numbers," he whispered. "Tanya won't be able to defend herself if we attack from all sides."

As all the other birds joined them, Rupert took a central position and outlined his plan of attack.

"The idea is to completely surround Tanya and give her no room for manoeuvre. Someone will have to get in very close to give her the ultimatum. If that doesn't work, we'll try chanting. And if that doesn't work, we attack with our beaks, and I don't mean gentle pecks! If it gets to that stage, she has to realise we really do mean business!"

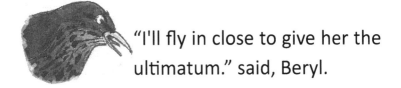

"I'll fly in close to give her the ultimatum." said, Beryl.

"No, I'll do that," interrupted Rob. "She's holding a robin, so it's my job. No arguments."

"Very well," agreed Rupert, "Sorry Beryl, but I'm sure you understand that's only right?" The female blackbird gave him a curt nod and turned to the robin.

"Take care Rob, she's got a wicked beak."

"Good advice, Beryl," agreed Rupert. "Now, remember everyone, we must completely surround her as Rob moves in. She must not, I repeat, must not, be allowed to move towards her nest. And do keep up the chanting, we all know what Tanya's like, she'll try to soft talk her way out, so don't give her the chance. Ready Rob?" Rob nodded. Rupert waved him off, counted to three, and gave the signal for the others to follow.

Tanya was rudely awakened to find

herself surrounded by a host of small garden birds. One of them hovering close to her eyes.

Rob went in even closer. So close, it almost looked as if he was going to land on Tanya's beak. Tanya blinked as the robin delivered the ultimatum in his usual, abrupt, no-nonsense style.

"Let go of him, or we'll duff you in!" he snarled.

Tanya moved her head from side to side, hoping to catch the robin with her razor-sharp beak.

"Go away little bird," she hissed. "Go away, before I make it two robins, in one day."

Rob bravely stood his ground and repeated the ultimatum. At the same time, all the birds picked up the chant.

"Let go of him
Let go of him

If you don't

WE'LL DUFF YOU IN!"

"Oh, really?" screeched Tanya.

"I'll eat this robin, just for starters. The rest of you, I'll have for afters."

The birds took no notice of Tanya's threats and began to chant.

"Drop that bird and stick to mice, if you don't you'll pay the price!"

The chanting reached a crescendo with half the birds shouting, "Let go of him!" and the other half shrieking, "Drop that bird!"

Then, led by Rob, they made a series of attacks, with the natural acrobats like Connie, Charlie and the other tits, swinging on Tanya's feathers to maintain an insistent and painful pecking action.

Tanya tried to move. She tried to shuffle towards her nest, but the birds closed in towards her eyes. It was too much. It was too painful for her to bear. With great reluctance, she let Leo go.

As Leo rolled off the bough and fluttered down to the branch below, Rupert called off the mobbing.

The birds escorted Leo back to his bird-station. He was shaken, but otherwise unscathed. He thanked all the birds for their help, especially, Bertie and Rob.

"You're most welcome," said Bertie.

"Anytime," said Rob, "but that don't mean you can dig into my worms. Got it?"

"I've got it," said Leo.

Throughout the ordeal with Tanya all he thought about was escaping from her clutches, but the mention of worms made him feel hungry again. However, the message from all the birds was the same. There was no food anywhere.

"If it goes on like this," groaned Bertie, "many of us will be hard pressed to survive the winter."

"I could go back into the house through my bedroom window," said Leo. "The food's stored on a shelf in the kitchen. If the door to my bedroom hasn't slammed shut, I could fly down the stairs and get there."

"Then what?" asked. Beryl. "I don't

want to be unkind, Leo, but you're a robin now, one of the smallest birds in the garden. You'll never be able to bring food out for us."

"Beryl's right," said Mr Crow. "And it's

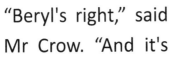

not just a matter of size, it's all to do with levers. As a boy you had long arms and legs. Those are levers. I've got a long beak which I can use as a lever, but a robin?"

"Oi! What's wrong with us robins?"

"Nothing, Rob," said Rupert soothingly. "Mr Crow is only pointing out that brave as robins are, Leo is not equipped to carry food out for us."

"I aim to bring it out through the cat flap," said Leo.

"You and whose army?" asked Beryl.

"I was thinking about getting my cat to help."

Bertie the bullfinch exploded with indignation.

"Your cat? May I remind you that you are surrounded by friends who put themselves in great danger to save you from the clutches of Tanya. A direct consequence of your being attacked by your own cat!"

"But Monty only attacked because he didn't know it was me. If you could tell him what's happened, I'm sure he would help."

"We don't speak to cats," said Basil.

"Only because we don't understand their language," said Rupert. "Could you help, Razz?"

Razz looked at Rupert and shook his head. "Afraid not, Rupert. As I've said before, I can't abuse my powers."

There was scuffling and a clucking sound from the bottom of the bird station.

"My sister could help."

The birds looked down to see one of the hens looking up at them.

"Go away!" trilled Beryl. "This is a private meeting. Wild birds only."

"Steady on Beryl," interceded Rupert. "At a time like this we need all the help we can get." He looked down at the hen. "Are you sure your sister can converse with the cat?"

"Yes, she's very good at languages. But I lay the biggest eggs."

Leo peered down at her.

"Did you know, some of them are double yolkers?"

"I'm not surprised."

"So you are Clarissa?"

"Of course. Who are you?"

"I'm Leo. The boy from the house. Where's Sophie?"

"Fast asleep on her perch. I heard all the commotion and came out to see what was going on."

"You're not surprised that I've been turned into a robin?"

"Nothing surprises me, I lay the biggest eggs. I'll get Sophie."

CHAPTER SEVEN

THROUGH THE CAT FLAP

Monty was in his bed, trying to sleep and forget. But, he could not forget! He could not forget that the robin looked at him, knew he was coming, yet ignored the danger; until it was too late! It was all very strange? He could not understand what birds said to each other, but the bullfinch was definitely warning the robin. The robin looked up, had the chance to fly away, but didn't. It even tried to speak to him. What did it say?

He went through everything, again and again, including how the owl snatched the robin away.

No wonder he couldn't get to sleep!

Then he heard something scratching at his cat flap! Reluctantly, he left the warmth of his bed to investigate and when he poked his head out into the cold night air, he got the shock of his life! All the birds in the garden were crowded around the back door. Sophie the hen was standing at the front with a robin sitting on her back. Sophie saw confusion in the cat's eyes and spoke quickly to reassure him.

"Don't be frightened, Monty. I'm here on behalf of the wild birds in your garden. They need your help."

The robin twittered and tweeted, but to Monty it was just that, twitters and tweets. He could understand what the humans said and he could understand Sophie, but not the other hen, Clarissa, or the wild birds.

Sophie spoke again.

"I know it will be difficult to believe, but the robin on my back is Leo the boy from the house. He's not cross that you pounced on him. He has been turned into a robin because he broke his promise to put food out for the birds. He wants you to help. He will tell me what it is he wants you to do and I will pass on his instructions. Do you understand?"

Monty nodded.

"Good. Now the first thing he wants you to do is come slowly out through your cat flap. When I tell you to stop, stop. Don't worry about Mr Crow and the stick he's carrying in his beak. The stick will be used to prop your cat flap open. The jackdaw helped him measure and cut it to the right length. When I tell you to stop, arch your back to push the cat flap as high as you can. They will wedge the stick in place. Do you understand? "

"Yes," said Monty.

"Are you ready."

"Yes," said Monty, nervously.

"Good," Said Sophie. "Now, come out

157

Monty glanced at the crow and Jackdaw. He was not keen on having them so close especially the crow with his long beak, but if Leo really was the robin, he had to do as he was told. He nodded his understanding. Under Leo's relayed instructions, Monty did exactly as he was told, but turned his head away from those dreadful beaks as the crow and jackdaw wedged the stick into position. He breathed a sigh of relief when he was told to go back into the kitchen.

With Leo on her back, Sophie followed and Leo immediately flew up to the worktop where the bird food was stored. A flash of red whizzed through the cat flap as Rob flew in to join him.

"What's the plan then, Leo? Ya know the others won't come into the house?"

"Razz said you would be the only one, so I was thinking of getting some suet fat balls out under the patio table as quickly as possible. They won't get buried under snow there."

"So, what d'ya want from me? I can't carry any of this lot any more than you can."

"I know that Rob, but with help from the hens, I'm hoping Monty will do the carrying for us. If you could ask Mr Crow and Jack to use their beaks to break up the suet balls into peckable sizes, that would be really helpful. Clarissa will come out to drag the nets about and spread the crumbs."

"Sounds good to me," said Rob, "but watch out, the hens are coming up!"

The two robins moved deftly to one side as Sophie and Clarissa, with wings flapping furiously, scrambled over the edge of the worktop. Leo hopped over to a row of suet fat balls. Grandpa Jim had stacked them within reaching distance for him, but that was as a boy, not a robin! He spoke to Sophie and Clarissa .

"We need to drag four of these over to the edge and drop them down for Monty. Sophie, can you please tell him to take them, one pack at a time, out onto the patio and leave them under the table. Mr Crow and Jack the jackdaw will be waiting to break them up with their beaks."

Sophie clucked her understanding as she helped Clarissa drag the first net of suet balls to the edge of the worktop.

When they had it overhanging the edge, she called down to Monty.

"Move to one side, Monty! First pack of fat balls coming down. Take it out and drop it under the patio table. Mr Crow and Jack are waiting. They're going to break them up with their beaks for the smaller birds. Come back as quickly as you can, there are three more packs to go."

With her back to the edge, Clarissa gave the net of fat balls a hefty kick and it tumbled off the worktop. Even as it was falling, Rob was speeding out through the cat flap to alert Mr Crow and Jack.

As Monty picked up the first net in his mouth, Sophie and Clarissa were dragging the second into position.

With that part of the operation going smoothly, Leo turned his thoughts towards the bird station. Monty would obviously not be able to fill the feeders, but he could spread some mixed seed and sunflower hearts on the bird table, under the sloping roof. He hopped up for a peek into the old rucksack.

There were half-used bags of seed in there, but the rucksack would be too big to go through Monty's cat flap. He would have to take one unopened bag through at a time, Sophie could tell him where to place them and how to tear them open with his claws. He shuddered at the thought of those claws. Phew!

When Leo followed Monty out through the cat flap on his last trip to the bird station, he paused to watch Clarissa dragging the last suet ball net around, spreading the crumbs for the smaller birds.

He briefly joined Binkie, Gwen, Connie and Charlie to peck up some crumbs. No one said anything, they were too busy eating. Mr Crow had warned them that a snow storm was on the way so they needed to eat as much as possible, before flying off to a place of shelter.

Taking an extra beak-full for luck, Leo flew to the bird station, where, supervised by Sophie, Monty was ripping a bag of sunflower hearts open. The hearts burst from the bag and spilled across the flat surface of the bird table to mingle with mixed seed from the previous delivery.

Leo asked Sophie to tell Monty to go back to his bed and if possible, knock the stick away so that his cat flap could close behind him.

As Sophie relayed his message to Monty, Leo looked up at the apple tree where Rupert was waiting patiently.

"All clear now, Rupert!" he twittered. Monty has ripped open the last bag."

"Thank you Leo, you've organised a great operation!"

"The least I could do," replied Leo, hastily flying down to join Sophie, as a mass of larger birds, made for the sunflower hearts and mixed seed.

"Thanks again Sophie, I don't know how I could have coped without your being able to speak Monty's language."

"I do have a way with languages," clucked, Sophie, modestly, "but Clarissa lays the biggest eggs."

As Sophie wandered off to meet her sister, it began to snow.

CHAPTER EIGHT

OVER THE RAINBOW

Leo flew up into the beech tree to look down over the garden. So much had happened, yet it was only just beginning to get light.

He could make out the shape of the house and if he squinted through the swirling snow, he thought he could see the windows. But then the wind blew and everything disappeared!

"It's a white-out!" Razz had joined him. "Well done, Leo. This blizzard will last for a couple of hours, but thanks to you, your feathered friends have enough food inside them to survive. But, there's more for you to learn, so come on, follow me!"

Leo had to take off quickly to keep up with Razz. They were flying into the teeth of the blizzard, yet Razz was going higher and higher. Leo called after him. "I don't think I can go any higher Razz. I'm flapping my wings like mad, but I'm not getting anywhere!"

"You are now," Razz shouted back. "Here comes our transport."

Leo looked up, down, left and right, but could see nothing. "What transport Razz?"

"Just let yourself go," said Razz, who had slowed to fly alongside him "Let yourself go, Leo, we have lift off!"

Leo was suddenly enveloped in a soft, comfortable, warm white mass. As he sank into it he felt a tremendous lift and surge forward.

"It is the only way to travel," said Razz, from somewhere in the soft whiteness.

"It's wonderful," said Leo, "but what is it?"

Razz's head suddenly popped up next to him.

"My boy, you are flying first class. You are flying in all the luxury and with the entire service one would expect on the back of.....a snow goose. Say hello to Lady Amelie."

"Hello, Lady Amelie," said Leo.

A snow white neck lifted into view. Then a bright orange beak, as the snow goose half turned her head towards them.

"Hi Razz, good to see you again. Who's the polite passenger?"

"This looks like a robin, but it's really a boy called Leo," answered Razz. I turned him into a robin because he broke a promise and forgot to feed the birds."

"Has Leo learnt his lesson?" asked the snow goose.

"Yes, Lady Amelie," replied Razz. "He has been very resourceful and managed to feed the birds before this blizzard arrived."

"That is good news, Razz. So you want me to fly Leo into springtime?"

"That would help him understand."

"Spring it is then," said Lady Amelie. She added something about warmth, plentiful food and good times, which Leo strained to hear as the words were snatched away by the wind when she turned her head to the front, increased her speed dramatically and flew directly into the blizzard.

"Take cover!" shouted Razz. "She

usually flies up through the hailstone belt!

Leo only just managed to burrow under the feathers of the snow goose, into the soft warm down, when he felt the first hailstone thump against her feathers.

"Thanks Razz."

"No problem, Leo. Now, you lie low until Lady Amelie gives you the all-clear. She'll take good care of you."

Leo began to panic. "You're not leaving me?"

"I can't fly with you into spring, Leo. I've got too much to do in the run-up to Christmas. See ya!"

Leo felt feathers move and a blast of cold air. Razz had gone!

He snuggled into the soft warm down and as the snow goose battled on through the storm, found a substantial feather to cling on to.

******

"Hi Leo!"

Leo woke-up. How long had he been asleep?

"Hi Leo, you can come out now, we're flying in sunshine."

He parted the feathers and looked out.

Lady Amelie lifted her long neck and turned her orange beak towards him.

"We're almost there, all I need is to find a rainbow. Will you help me look for one?"

"What do you need a rainbow for?" asked Leo.

"You've been a very good boy. Razz has asked me to fly you into spring, but to do that, I need to catch a rainbow. Let me know if you see one."

"I'll keep a look out," said Leo, wondering what Lady Amelie would do with a rainbow if they found one. Grandpa Jim had told him that finding a pot of gold at the end of the rainbow was an old wives' tale. It was impossible to find the end of a rainbow, but Leo did not want to upset the snow goose by telling her. He looked to the right, then to the left. There was no point in looking straight ahead, because she would surely see one if it was there. But as he transferred his gaze back to the right, he caught sight of a rainbow. It was lower than them and painted a big colourful arc across the horizon.

"There, Lady Amelie!"

"Where?" asked the snow goose. looking to the left and then to the right!

"In front of you!" shouted Leo.

"I can't see anything," said Lady

Amelie, in the sort of voice grandpa Jim used when he was joking with him.

Leo laughed. "It's there, Lady Amelie! Almost below us!"

"Ah, yes. I see it now. We're going to have to dive to chase that rainbow. Hold tight!" The snow goose rolled over into a power dive, and in a most unladylike manner shouted, "Rainbow ahead! Chase it! Catch it!"

Leo was convinced Lady Amelie was close to the speed of sound as they hurtled down through the clouds. Then, without any warning, it was brakes on "How does she do it?" he wondered, sliding halfway up her neck. When he slid down again he found the white back of the snow goose covered in a spectrum of colour.

"We're in the rainbow now," said Lady Amelie, "time for you to leave."

"What? Fly down the rainbow?"

The snow goose laughed. "Why would a little boy want fly down a rainbow when he can slide? That must be the way."

Lady Amelie slid her bright orange beak underneath Leo and lifted him carefully onto the top of the rainbow.

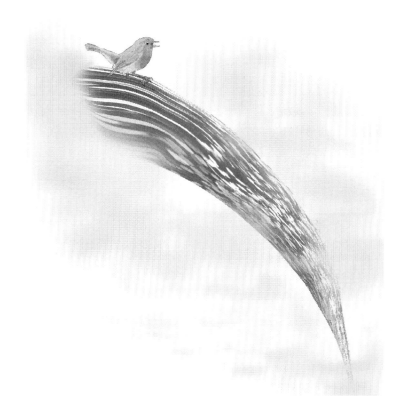

Leo sat for a few seconds, then slowly began to slide.

"Don't forget to spread your wings when you see the ground!" shouted the snow goose.

"I won't!" Leo shouted back. "Thank you Lady Amelie. Thank you very much!"

"You are most welcome!" shouted Lady Amelie, as she zoomed off into the clouds.

CHAPTER NINE

THE SHOW IS OVER

Remembering that he was a robin, Leo lifted his tail and slid down the rainbow on his rump. He adjusted speed and direction by digging into the rainbow with the back claw on each foot and as he did so, a shower of multi-coloured droplets washed over him, creating trails which spread out from the rainbow, turning the sky into a great canvas of vivid colour. He looked up to admire his work and then..."Crikey! The ground! It's coming up fast!"

Leo spread his wings just in time and landed with a bump at the end of the rainbow.

There was no pot of gold, but as far as he could see, the rainbow was passing through the roof of his bird station. He was lying in lush grass and daisies, and thinking about making an effort to fly up to see if there was any food, when he heard a familiar voice.

"Sitting at the end of that rainbow, with all that colour washing over you, makes you look more like me than a robin."

It was Razz! Leo hopped around in excitement, trying to find out where the voice had come from.

"Up here Leo, on the bird-bath. Hurry, or you'll miss the show."

Leo flew up and hovered excitedly by the bird-bath. The last time he saw it, it was solid with ice and covered with snow. "You'll never guess what, Razz. Lady Amelie put me on the top of a rainbow and I used it as a giant slide."

"I know, Leo. Now calm down and perch next to me, or you'll miss the show."

"What show?"

Before Razz could answer, a song thrush spoke to them from the Apple tree.

It was Rupert! Leo really was back in his own garden, but it all looked so different.

Trees were in blossom and spring flowers were blooming. The garden was a riot of colour, enhanced by the presence of the rainbow.

Rupert coughed and then spoke rather formally. "Welcome, Razz. Welcome Leo. May I escort you to your reserved tree space?"

"But of course," said Razz. "Delighted to see you again Rupert."

They followed the song thrush into the apple tree to a section of bough, framed by blossom, which provided a clear view towards the garden and bird station. Rupert perched on an outer branch and spoke in a loud voice. "Birds of Camber Garden, will you please welcome our guests of honour."

The apple tree and nearby bushes and shrubs, erupted with a chorus of chirping, twittering, whistling and clapping of wings. Looking around, Leo could see all his old friends. Goldie was perched with another goldfinch on an outer twig. Beryl and Basil were surrounded by young blackbirds. Rob was perched on the garden roller with another robin. All the tits, including Connie, were swinging around on one of the higher branches. Lower down, Bertie was surrounded by his family of bull finches.

On a branch nearby stood Binkie, watching over a clutch of house sparrows. The tree and surrounding area was packed with birds making a tremendous din, overlooked by Mr Crow, who had come down to one of the lower branches of his beech tree for the occasion.

"I think you'd better take a bow, or they'll never stop," shouted Razz.

"Why me?" yelled Leo.

"Because, this is their way of saying thank you for looking after them throughout the winter."

"Yes, we all came through, thanks to you," shouted Bertie. "Splendid work, absolutely splendid."

"But I've not done anything yet," protested Leo. "I forgot to feed you when Grandpa Jim went away. Don't you remember?"

"Yes, but you've looked after them well ever since. Just listen to them," said Razz.

"But I'm still a robin, how could I possibly have looked after them?"

Razz reached out and touched Leo with his wing. "You have been allowed a glimpse into the future. You can take it from me, you have helped these birds through one of the hardest winters on record. This is the only chance they'll have of saying thank you, in a way you can understand. Now, take that bow!"

Leo stepped shyly forward and the noise grew louder and louder. Eventually, Rupert held up his wings to call for silence. Everything went very quiet, and Rupert looked towards a woodpecker, clinging to the trunk of the pear tree and said.

"Mr Woodpecker.....if you please!"

The woodpecker launched into the most amazing drum solo. It reached a crescendo, and then faded away to nothing. The woodpecker's head was still moving, but there was no sound. Everyone strained to hear.....and there it was the lightest, softest drum roll you could possibly imagine. Gradually, it became louder...and louder. Then, scurrying action drew attention to the oldest apple tree in the garden. Spiders were running into position to pull on silken threads. And as they pulled, gossamer curtains parted to reveal......a stage!

"What's going on?" whispered Leo.

"They've laid on a great show," whispered Razz. "Watch carefully, you will never see another show like it."

Razz was right. It was the most fantastic show Leo had ever seen.

As the drum roll ended, Jack the jackdaw strode onto the stage. With his shiny black and grey plumage, it looked for all the world as if he was in evening dress. Jack asked for applause for the woodpecker's marvellous drum solo and got it.

Then, to get the show started, he introduced, 'The Linnets' a chorus line of young linnets, who kicked their legs up in perfect time to music provided by a band of assorted warblers.

They were followed by Harry Hoopoe, a continental comedian.

Harry looked so comical, he hardly had to say anything to get a laugh and when he did tell a joke, you could not hear the end of it, because he was laughing so much.

"That's the secret of his success," whispered Razz. "He never bothers with new jokes, because no one has ever managed to hear the end of his old ones."

Rupert was next on the bill, with a wonderful 'song thrush ballad'.

He received a tremendous reception and ended up singing three songs.

The blue tits did a tumbling act, followed by a hawfinch, who juggled three fruit stones with his massive beak.

As a surprise, he cracked them one by one and juggled with the pieces as he ate the kernels.

Gwen the wren was the female solo singer. She was amazing. How could such a small bird have such a loud voice? Loud, yet clear and sweet.

Binkie and another house sparrow were a comedy double act.

Followed by Beryl and Basil singing a love duet.

All too soon, the show was over and Jack called all the performers back on stage for the finale. They all sang "Food Glorious Food" which they dedicated to Leo. As they finished, the spiders rushed out to close the gossamer curtains. The audience cheered like mad and the cast took two curtain calls.

It should have been three, but the spiders, who knew very well that some of the birds would not mind them as a snack, decided they had risked enough, and disappeared back into the woodwork.

When the applause died down, Jack came out through the curtains. "Birds of Camber Garden and special guests," he boomed. "We hope you enjoyed our little show, but, your entertainment is not quite over. Rupert, as we all know, is a great organiser."

This brought hoots of twittering, chirping and whistling from the audience. The song thrush smiled and gave a little bow.

"And!" Jack raised his voice to shout over the din. "And, he has laid on something very special for us today. It is a tribute to his persuasive skills, for they have never given a display over our garden before. However, I can assure you that even as I speak, they're about to fly into view. They are.....The Starlings!"

The announcement was greeted by ooooohs and aaaahs and all the birds looked up.

"What's so special about starlings?" asked Leo.

"Ah, when you see them in small groups nothing in particular," repied Razz. "But when they get together in hundreds, or even thousands, they become the most amazing aerial display team you'll ever see. Here they come!"

The starlings approached like a fast moving cloud. Hundreds of them, flying in perfect formation. When they were directly over the garden, they looped the loop without one bird out of position. Then, they peeled off in groups and flew away in different directions.

"Is that it," asked Leo.

But before Razz could answer, they were back, swooping in low from all four corners of the garden at a terrific speed. They joined together as one formation again above the bird-table and climbed vertically until they disappeared into the clouds.

Heads turned this way and that. "Was that the end?"

"No, there they are!" shouted Binkie. "They're coming down the rainbow!"

Leo looked up through the apple tree, and sure enough, there they were, diving down the rainbow, straight for the bird station. They were in groups of perhaps one hundred or so. The last group wheeled onto the top of the rainbow, as the first pulled out of their dive and whistled over the old apple tree, taking with them a trail of red from the rainbow. The next group zoomed out over the oak tree, leaving a trail of blue. The next over the house trailing yellow, and so it continued with each group of starlings taking a colour from the rainbow. By the time they finished, the sky above the garden looked like a giant Catherine wheel.

As the birds whistled and cheered, the rainbow and streaks of colour splashed across the sky, began to fade.

"Time to go," whispered Razz. He flew down to the bird-bath and Leo followed. They perched facing each other, in the centre of the fading rainbow.

"Should I say goodbye?"

"What for?" said Razz. "They're the birds in your garden; you'll be seeing them every day."

"But not as a robin," said Leo.

"That's true," said Razz, "but they'll be relying on you for survival, so you must go back to feed them."

The birds were still looking skywards, in case the starlings came back.

"Here we go then," said Razz. "Hold onto your feathers!"

Leo felt as if he was being pulled into the air, and he was!

The rainbow had become a giant

straw and he was being sucked up the middle of it.

Bright colours flashed past at a tremendous speed. Then they turned darker, dark reds, purples and blues, until suddenly, everything went black and he seemed to be floating in space. Then, he began to fall, tumbling head over heels. He tried spreading his wings, but it made no difference, he was completely out of control. He cried out in panic. "Razz, help me! I'm falling......Raaaaaaaaazzzz!!"

Leo landed with a surprisingly light bump. He opened his eyes and the first thing he saw was carpet and a pattern which looked familiar. He looked up at a bed and bedside lamp which also seemed familiar, as did the curtains. He was back in his own room! He had fallen out of bed!

"Oh no," he groaned. "It was all a dream.....only a dream."

"Oh no it wasn't," said a voice from the window.

Leo scrambled to his feet and rushed across the room. Snow was blowing in through the open window and perched on the ledge, sheltering from a raging blizzard, was the razzdazz oriole.

Razz looked up at Leo. "It wasn't a dream," he said. "It all happened. Now, get out and feed those feathered friends of yours, Grandpa Jim will be back tomorrow."

"In all this snow?"

"The snow will stop in about an hour but he's delaying his return to bring your great-aunt Libby with him. Oh and by the way. I've arranged for your father to be home for Christmas."

Leo could not help but burst out laughing. "Even you can't do that, Razz. Dad's on a contract!"

"Well now," said Razz, his beak tweaking into a gentle smile. "I could have sworn I made arrangements for the work on that contract to finish early."

THE END

When Razz disappeared in a swirling blaze of colour, Leo quickly put outside clothes over his pyjamas and crept down to the kitchen. It was warm and the cat flap was closed. Monty woke up and seemed surprised but pleased to see him. He watched as Leo put extra bags of birdseed into the rucksack and hoisted it onto his back, but he was not interested enough to follow him out into the swirling snow.

Leo ignored the discarded netting from the fat ball packs under the patio table. He would clear those up later. The bird feeders were his top priority.

As he approached the bird station, Rob flew to meet him. Leo had several meal worms at the ready and Rob twittered as he pulled them out from his woollen mitten. Leo laughed.

"I know what you're saying, Rob. It's

about blinking time!"

Rob twittered again as he flew up to perch on the safety rail of the climbing frame which had been converted into Leo's Bird Station.

Leo soon had the first feeder filled and as he turned the old bike pedal to set it off towards the post, all his old friends clustered around. Their twitters and tweets encouraged him to work quickly and when all the feeders were out on the line, he turned his attention to the flat surface of the bird table, brushing off the loose snow and piling it high with sunflower hearts and a wild bird seed mixture.

He caused a mini-avalanche when he used the slide and had to struggle out from a pile of snow, to watch the birds, his friends, as they clustered around the bird station. Jack the jackdaw was feeding from the bird table with Beryl and Basil the blackbirds and Rupert the song thrush.

Connie the coal tit was furiously pulling sunflower hearts from a feeder and dropping them for Bertie the bullfinch who was waiting below. Leo wondered if Connie was helping because she knew Bertie had a dodgy wing? It wouldn't surprise him, the birds seemed to look after each other. Mobbing Tanya to save him from her clutches was a good example. He shuddered at the thought. Time to pull himself together! There was more work to be done.

His mother came down to the kitchen as he filled a small watering can with hot water.

"You're up and about early, Leo."

"Wanted to make sure the birds were alright, Mum."

"And are they?"

"Seemed pleased to see me," said Leo. "I'm about to thaw the bird-bath. Do you want me to take anything out for the hens?"

"That's a nice thought, darling. I have a long list of patients to call and that will be very helpful. I'll get some hot mash ready. What do you intend to do for the rest of the morning?"

"I'm going to log some bird sightings and colour-in some of the drawings for Grandpa."

"Anything exciting?"

"A redwing. And, I caught a glimpse of a very colourful bird, but I don't know what that could be," he lied.

"Probably a parakeet," said his mother. "A lot of those have escaped into the wild."

When Leo took the hot mash to the hens, they clucked as he opened the door and stepped into their run. He was disappointed to find that he could not understand what Sophie was saying, but thanked them for their help anyway. Sophie seemed to understand, even if she did answer with her beak full and Clarissa strutted and preened when he told her it was common knowledge that she laid the biggest eggs.

After breakfast, his mother cleared away and suggested that he completed his drawings on the kitchen table. As she went into her study, Leo worked on colouring the drawings he had logged in the note book, Grandpa Jim had given him. On the last page, he recorded the sighting of the red-wing. Then, satisfied with his work, he went to the beginning and compared what he had seen against the notes and drawings in Grandpa Jim's well thumbed exercise book. Strangely, the last entry in his book was also for a red-wing. He looked at the drawing. Perhaps he could cheat and copy from it? Then he noticed something strange. The last page in the book had been folded and pasted down as a flap. He carefully lifted a

corner, peeled it back and was surprised to find, a drawing of Razz! Under the coloured drawing, Grandpa Jim had printed:
RAZZDAZZ ORIOL : RARE WINTER VISITOR.

Leo folded the flap back in place and looked up as his mother rushed into the kitchen.

"Wonderful news, Leo. Grandpa Jim is driving up with Great Aunt Libby tomorrow! And guess what?"

"Don't tell me," said Leo. "Dad's coming home for Christmas!"

His mother looked at him in astonishment.

"How could you possibly know that? I've only just finished talking to your father on the telephone"

Leo gave her a cheeky grin. "You're not going to believe this Mum. A little bird told me!"

FOLLOW THE AUTHOR

Find out more about Peter Tye and his children's stories by visiting his website.

www. petertye.co.uk

Printed in Great
Britain
by Amazon